# TINY CRAB
## IS A TIDY CRAB

For Tidy-up Champion,

Finley Breen:

'Littering is Rubbish!'

P. B.

**SIMON & SCHUSTER**

First published in Great Britain in 2022 by Simon & Schuster UK Ltd

1st Floor, 222 Gray's Inn Road, London, WC1X 8HB

Text and illustrations copyright © 2022 Paula Bowles

The right of Paula Bowles to be identified as the author and illustrator of this work

has been asserted by her in accordance with the Copyright,

Designs and Patents Act, 1988 • All rights reserved, including

the right of reproduction in whole or in part in any form

A CIP catalogue record for this book is available

from the British Library upon request

ISBNs: 978-1-4711-9178-7 (HB) 978-1-4711-9179-4 (PB) 978-1-4711-9177-0 (eB)

Printed in China

1 3 5 7 9 10 8 6 4 2

MIX
Paper from
responsible sources
FSC
www.fsc.org
FSC® C144853

# TINY CRAB
## IS A TIDY CRAB

### PAULA BOWLES

**SIMON & SCHUSTER**

London   New York   Sydney   Toronto   New Delhi

Once upon a beautiful beach, under a tall palm tree,
Tiny Crab watched the waves go swoosh,

swash,

swiiiiiishhhhh . . .

Tiny Crab loved surfing,

building tall
sandcastles,

and chilling in the
shade with a cool
coconut smoothie.

But most of all, Tiny Crab loved caring for his beach.
He always tidied up at the end of each day,
because Tiny Crab is a tidy crab.

One day he wondered,
"This is such a special sand pit,
wouldn't it be super to share it!"

So he invited a friend to visit.

And the next day, Seagull arrived.

"Thanks for the invite!" he squawked, then,

"I hope you don't mind, I invited some friends too . . ."

"Oh!" squeaked Tiny Crab.
"Just look at everyone!"

He was a bit surprised to see
so many animals on his beach,
but he was happy to share.

He smiled and waved, although no one saw him.
So instead, Tiny Crab watched them all have fun.

There were beach parties and barbecues,

kite-flying and kayaking.

Everyone had a GREAT TIME!

Soon, it was time for the other animals
to go, but when they left . . .

"Oh! My beach is a bin!
Ah, my head's in a spin!"
cried Tiny Crab, as he gazed
at the mess left behind.

So Tiny Crab tidied up,

snapping things
from under his feet,

and getting his beach just right.

Until, finally, he was finished,
just in time to watch the sunrise,

when suddenly . . .

. . . All the animals
came back

BEACH BUS

bringing even more friends . . .

"Oh, hello!" waved Tiny Crab, but nobody saw him
and nobody heard him. He sighed, but smiled,
"Well, it's nice to have guests . . .
if they remember their mess!"

This time there was surfing and snorkelling,
and sun-bathing and swimming.

But when the end of the day came
and the animals went home again,

Tiny Crab gasped, "My beach!!! It's a bin AGAIN!"

So as the tide came in and the sun went down,
Tiny Crab tidied, snip-snapping things up
from under his feet . . .

finally getting his beach nice.

But the next day the animals came back, they brought
even more friends, and there was stuff EVERYWHERE!

There were beach huts, snack shacks, and inflatable things.
And there were really long queues for ice-pops
and ice-creams and tall water flumes!

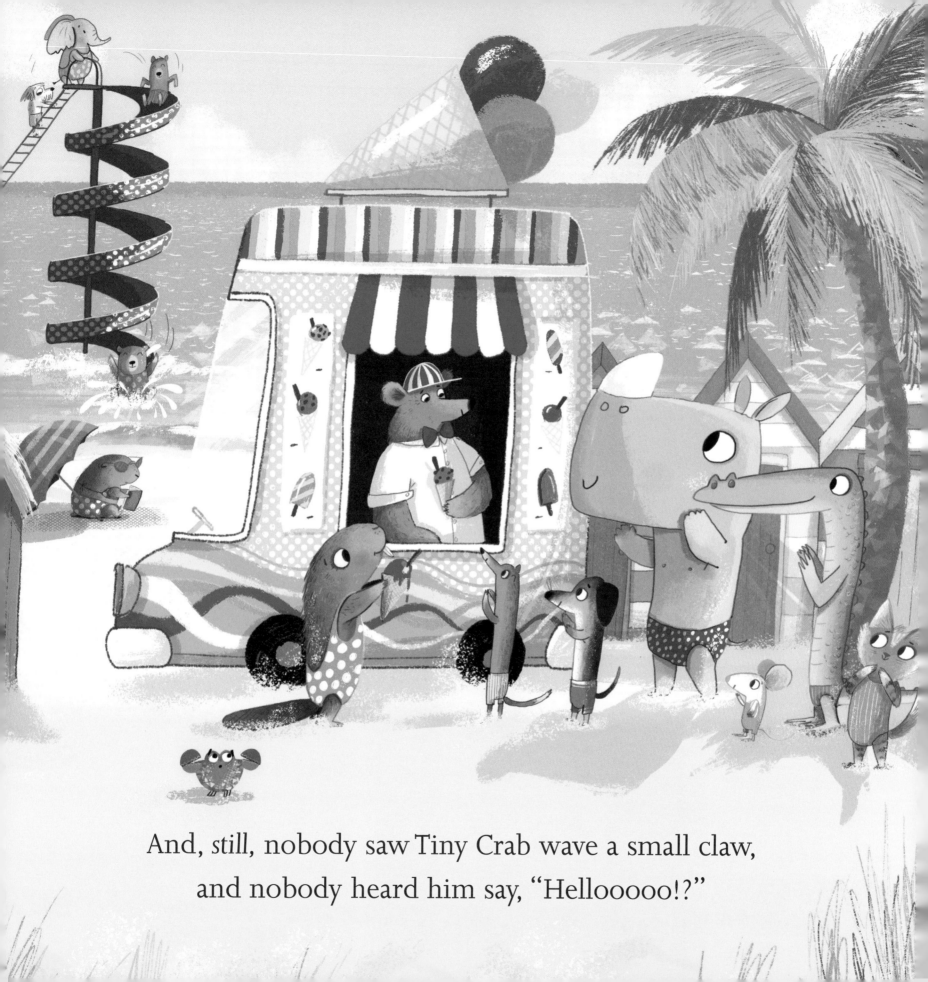

And, *still*, nobody saw Tiny Crab wave a small claw,
and nobody heard him say, "Hellooooo!?"

Tiny Crab watched the animals dropping their rubbish
and he muttered to himself, "Not again!!"

Then Tiny Crab scuttled
around, tidying
up the beach . . .

moving
things about

while nobody
noticed, until . . .

THIS BEACH IS MY HOME!
IT ISN'T A NICE WAY
TO SHARE IF YOU DON'T
TIDY UP YOUR RUBBISH!

The animals couldn't believe their eyes and ears!
They suddenly saw the beach was a HUGE mess.
"We're so sorry," they gasped.

"We promise to keep it clean from now on!"
And together they all tidied up.

With so many paws, and so many claws,
they had it clean in no time.

When they finished, they all
sat upon the beautiful beach

and watched the waves go
swoosh, swash, swiiiiiishhhhh . . .

And this time, when they said goodbye,
they left something behind again . . .

. . . but it was just their
paw prints in the sand.